RAINA
AND THE
LAZY SNOWFLAKES

Written by Sophia Diogene

Illustrated by Kayla Hargrove

For all the quiet little girls that sit and dream by a window.

Waiting for the first snowflake is so boring! Just when you think it's freezing enough for those crystal flakes to sprinkle down like a giant salt shaker...

1

...all you get is the cold roaring wind.

"Mama?"

"Yes, Raina."

"When will-"

"Ohhh no! Are you going to ask me about the snow, again?
That's the third time today."

"Well, I was just-"

3

"Raina, I haven't the slightest clue when the snow will get here. We'll simply have to wait our turn."

"But-"

"Patience, Raina. The weather is something we don't have the power to control. Those crystal flakes will fall when nature decides and no sooner." 4

Raina stumped away and tightened her little lips.

"Don't you stump those tiny toes away, little miss. At least not without taking one of my famous cinnamon pumpkin cookies," Mama said with a warm smile. Raina circled back, reached for a cookie, and smiled as Mama kissed her forehead.

"They will come. Just try to be patient and before you know it the snow will be tickling that button nose," promised Mama as she spun Raina in the air.

In her bedroom, Raina held a cookie in her hand with crumbs falling all over her snowflake drawing.

"The most amazing thing I learned about snowflakes at school is that because of the way they are created, no two flakes are alike! Each flake has a unique pattern. A snowflake is born by falling through layers of air.

As it falls, each layer of the flake is formed at a different temperature with different amounts of moisture to create a very unique crystal flake every time!"

Raina heard her father calling at the foot of the stairs. She threw her crayons and cookies in the air and rushed down to greet him.

She leapt into his arms, and he nearly took a tumble.

"Ha ha! Well, aren't you a ball of energy today!"

Raina smiled as she tightly clung her little arms around his neck.

"You know, Raina, Mama says you've been a bit of a handful about the snow today."
Raina hung her head in shame. She knew Mama was busy making the cookies for the
school bake sale, and she probably should have been a bit quieter today.

"But Daddy-!"

"No buts, young lady. Now, up the stairs you go..."

Daddy gently placed Raina on a step, and she feared she was being sent back to stay in her room until dinner for misbehaving.

But then something unexpected! Daddy knelt down and whispered in her ear, "...to find your boots and coat! I'm taking you and your little brother to Rockefeller Center for a little ice skating." Raina's eyes were full of excitement and curiosity again. She had never been to Rockefeller Center before!

She shot up like a jackrabbit and ran up the stairs to her bedroom closet.

Up into the air went her fuzzy green and pink polka dot slippers. Zip across the room was the curly haired doll with the missing shoe. Raina searched and searched for her warmest matching socks, but when she found one she couldn't find the other.

"Raina! We're all set to go!"

Raina pulled on the only warm socks she found along with her sweater, boots, coat, and flew down the stairs. There she found Mama holding her favorite scarf and waiting to see everyone off.

Mama, covered in flour, waved goodbye to everyone as they climbed into a cab.

Raina had a full day of fun with her baby brother and Daddy. They saw and skated under the sparkling branches of the decorated Christmas tree. Raina stopped and looked up at the 89-foot tall tree. She wondered in amazement at how the tree got there. How did they get all the way to the top with little ornaments, lights and that beautiful star? 25

Each branch looked as though it were holding a party for a thousand golden fairies. Raina took a deep breath in and could smell the wood and pinecones from the silent green giant above her.

After skating and hot cocoa at Mr. Kohler's Chocolate and Candy Shop, Daddy carried a sleeping Raina home. But as she slept soundly on his shoulders, she felt something cold on her nose.

Raina opened her eyes and saw winter's first snowflakes finally cascading all around her.

She held out her little hand, looked at the sparkling little pile and said with the biggest

smile, "Well, it's about time!"

Made in the USA
Columbia, SC
14 February 2020